Esme
the Ice Cream
Fairy

To all ice cream lovers everywhere

Special thanks to Sue Mongredien

No part of this publication may be reproduced, stored in a retrieval system, or transmitted in any form or by any means, electronic, mechanical, photocopying, recording, or otherwise, without written permission of the publisher. For information regarding permission, write to Rainbow Magic Limited, c/o HIT Entertainment, 830 South Greenville Avenue, Allen, TX 75002-3320.

ISBN 978-0-545-60532-8

12 11 10 9 8 7 6 5 4 3 2 1   14 15 16 17 18 19/0

Printed in the U.S.A.   40

This edition first printing, March 2014

Esme
the Ice Cream Fairy

by Daisy Meadows

SCHOLASTIC INC.

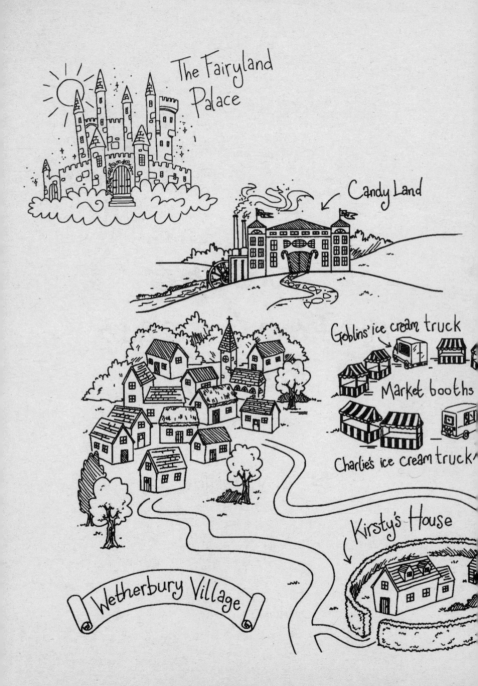

The Fairyland Palace

Candy Land

Goblins' ice cream truck

Market booths

Charlie's ice cream truck

Kirsty's House

Wetherbury Village

Jack Frost's
Ice Castle

Fair

The Park

Candy
Shop

High St.

I have a plan to make a mess
And cause the fairies much distress.
I'm going to take their charms away
And make my dreams come true today!

I'll build a castle made of sweets,
And ruin the fairies' silly treats.
I just don't care how much they whine,
Their cakes and candies will be mine!

Contents

Ice Cream Emergency   1

Enter Esme!   13

A Cool Pool?   27

Turning Green   35

Splat!   47

Trapped!   57

Ice Cream Emergency

"Bye, Aunt Helen," said Kirsty Tate, hugging her aunt. "It was really nice to see you again."

"Thanks for all the candy," added Rachel Walker, Kirsty's best friend. She was staying with Kirsty over spring break.

Aunt Helen smiled at them. "My

pleasure," she said. "I'm sorry they weren't as good as usual, though."

Kirsty's aunt had the best job in the world: She worked at Candy Land, the treat factory just outside of Wetherbury. She'd come to have lunch with the Tates that day, bringing a big bag of Candy Land goodies for everyone. Unfortunately, the candy had tasted terrible. Something had gone horribly wrong!

The girls were disappointed—but their dismay had quickly turned to excitement when their friend Honey the Candy Fairy magically appeared in Kirsty's bedroom. She told them that strange things had been happening at her Fairyland Candy Factory, and asked if they'd help her.

Kirsty and Rachel hadn't hesitated for a second. Of course they'd help — they loved going to Fairyland! And so they'd been swept up in another wonderful fairy adventure, this time with Honey and her team of Sugar and Spice Fairies. It had been the most perfect start to the week, Rachel thought, smiling to herself.

The girls, Aunt Helen, and Kirsty's mom were now standing outside Tracy Twist's candy shop in Wetherbury, where Aunt Helen was catching the bus back to work. "I hope

everything's working the way it should at Candy Land again," she said. "At least the lollipops were good."

"The lollipops were *delicious*," Kirsty replied, with a secret wink at Rachel. Earlier that day, the  two of them had met Lisa the Lollipop Fairy. They had a thrilling time tracking down her magic lollipop charm, which had been stolen by wicked Jack Frost. Lisa used her magic charm to make lollipops everywhere lickable, and while it was missing they had tasted horrible. Luckily, Kirsty and Rachel had helped Lisa get it back. Now all the lollipops were yummier than ever!

"Good," Aunt Helen said. "I left a

special surprise for you back at your
house, which I hope you like, too." She
grinned at the girls. "Ah, here comes my
bus. Good-bye, all of you. Thanks for a
lovely lunch!"

"Bye!"
chorused
Kirsty, Rachel,
and Mrs. Tate,
waving to Aunt
Helen as the bus
drove away
slowly.

"I wonder what the
surprise is," Kirsty said
once the bus was out of sight.

"Knowing Aunt Helen, it's something
really good," Mrs. Tate said with a
smile.

Rachel smiled, too, and felt a fluttery feeling inside at the thought of a surprise waiting for them. Whenever she and Kirsty got together, life was always full of surprises!

They headed back toward Kirsty's house. As they walked through the market square, Rachel found herself looking out for more fairies. Honey had a team of seven Sugar and Spice Fairies, who helped her create delicious treats using their special magic charms. Unfortunately, Jack Frost had decided that he wanted all their yummy treats for himself. He was planning to

build a gigantic Candy Castle! He had ordered his goblins to steal the magic charms so he could make the best treats ever. Unfortunately, while the charms were away from their fairy owners, candy and treats didn't look or taste as good as usual!

Even worse, this had all happened just before the fairies' annual Treat Day! This was the day when Queen Titania and King Oberon gave every fairy a basket full of treats as a special thank-you for their hard work all year. It looked like those baskets would remain empty—unless the girls could help the Sugar and Spice Fairies get their magic charms back from the goblins.

Kirsty was scanning the market booths closely, too. "Mom, could we look

around a little, please?" she asked. "We can meet you at home later, if that's okay." The Tates only lived a few streets away, and it was a safe walk back.

"That's fine," Mrs. Tate said with a smile, and took her wallet out of her purse. "Here," she went on. "Let me give you some spending money, just in case you see something you like."

"Thank you!" Rachel said.

"We'll be back in an hour," Kirsty promised.

The girls said good-bye and made their

way through the square. It was lined with all kinds of booths, selling jewelery, toys, local vegetables, and brightly colored candles. Then they spotted an ice cream truck, and Kirsty licked her lips. It was a sunny day, and she could really go for a delicious, cool ice cream cone.

"They look good," Rachel said, studying the sign propped up near the truck. "Caramel Crunch—*mmm*, my favorite."

"Chocolate Swirl sounds yummy, too," Kirsty said, her tummy rumbling. "Ooh, and Mint Chocolate Chip. How will we decide?"

The man in the truck smiled. He was wearing a white uniform and hat, and had a name tag with CHARLIE printed  on it. "Would you like to try a few flavors?" he asked. "It might help you make up your minds."

"Yes, please!" both girls replied.

"No problem," Charlie said. He gave them each a tiny spoonful of Strawberries and Cream, then another of Mint Chocolate Chip.

Rachel put the pink strawberry ice cream in her mouth, expecting it to dissolve deliciously on her tongue. Instead, it felt like a flavorless lump of ice. "Oh!" she said in surprise.

Kirsty was about to try the Mint Chocolate Chip, but before she had even put the spoon to her lips, the ice cream melted to liquid and dripped onto the ground. Strange!

A horrible thought occurred to both girls at the same time. "This must be because of Jack Frost!" Kirsty whispered. "He's even ruining ice cream!"

Enter Esme!

Another customer approached the ice cream truck and began giving Charlie a long, complicated order. Kirsty and Rachel seized the chance to slip away for a minute.

"Let's look around the truck," Rachel suggested in a low voice. "We might find

another one of the Sugar and Spice Fairies."

"Good idea!" Kirsty agreed, feeling a flutter of excitement at the thought. Two fairy adventures in the same day would be a real treat!

The girls searched eagerly around the truck, hoping to see a sparkle, which would mean that a fairy was nearby. But even though they looked at every part of the truck, from top to bottom and front to back, they spotted nothing unusual.

They wandered around the front of the truck again, where the customer was just leaving. Her hands were full of ice cream cones, none of which looked very tasty.

"Goodness!" Charlie exclaimed. "That lady cleaned me right out of Chocolate Chunk. Give me a minute, girls. I'll just pop into the back to get some more."

Charlie vanished into the back of the truck, and the girls stood waiting at the counter.

"I'm not sure I actually *want* an ice cream cone now," Rachel whispered. "Should we go somewhere else?"

Kirsty was just about to agree when an extra paper hat on the counter, like the one Charlie was wearing, caught her eye. "Look!" she cried. "That hat! It's glowing!" Rachel's eyes widened in excitement. She carefully lifted the hat. Then she beamed as a tiny fairy fluttered out and landed on a stack of cones, her feet dangling over the edge. The fairy had long black hair and wore a pastel-striped

top, bright yellow
pants, and pink
sneakers. The stripes
on her shirt
reminded Rachel
of Raspberry
Ripple ice cream!

"Hello there,"
said the fairy in a
high, tinkling
voice. "I'm Esme
the Ice Cream Fairy!
We met earlier, in Fairyland."

"Hello again, Esme. I'm Kirsty, and
this is Rachel," Kirsty reminded her.

"And we're really glad to see you,"
Rachel said. She checked to make sure
that Charlie wasn't back before adding,

"The ice cream from this truck is *awful*!"

Esme nodded, looking serious. "It isn't very good," she agreed. "And it's all because Jack Frost took my magic ice cream cone charm. I have a feeling that the goblins are somewhere in this market with my 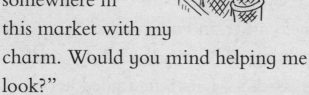 charm. Would you mind helping me look?"

"Mind? Not a bit!" Kirsty said eagerly. "We'd love to!"

"Here we go," Charlie said just then,

reappearing
with a large
tub of chocolate
ice cream in
his arms. He
opened the
freezer and
popped it
inside. While

his head was hidden in the
freezer, Esme leaped off the cones and
fluttered into Rachel's skirt pocket.

Charlie lifted his head, looking
confused. "That's strange," he said. "All
my ice cream seems to have melted. How
could that have happened?"

"Oh, no," Rachel said.

"I'm sorry, girls," he went on. "Maybe

this freezer is broken. I'm afraid I'll have to close the truck while I investigate."

"Thanks anyway," Kirsty said. "I hope you can figure it out soon." She glanced at Rachel as they turned away. "I hope *we* can figure it out, really," she added in a whisper.

Esme poked her head out of Rachel's pocket, and the sun sparkled on her dark, wavy hair. "Let's keep a lookout for anything unusual," she said. "We have  to stop Jack Frost and the goblins, or there won't be any ice cream for Treat Day—the day after tomorrow!"

The girls wandered through the

market, watching carefully for anything strange going on. One lady selling jewelery had a hood hiding her face. Kirsty looked closely, wondering if she was a goblin in disguise. Then the lady gave her customer a beaming smile, and Kirsty glanced away. No—she definitely *wasn't* a goblin. No goblin was ever that nice and friendly!

Next was a booth selling wooden toys. Rachel narrowed her eyes suspiciously when she saw that the man there had a baseball cap pulled low over his face. Was *that* a goblin?

Then he lifted
his hat and
scratched his
head, and
Rachel saw
that his skin
was pink rather
than goblin-green.
No — he wasn't a goblin, either!

"Maybe the ice cream just melted in
the sun," Kirsty said doubtfully. "Maybe
Charlie's freezer really *did* break."

Esme shook her head. "No," she said.
"I'm sure I can sense goblins around here
somewhere. Let's keep looking."

"Hey, Kirsty," came a voice just then,
and the girls turned to see two boys
approaching.

"Hi, Liam! Hi, Jamal!" Kirsty said. "This is my friend Rachel. Liam and Jamal go to my school," she explained.

Rachel said hi, and then her gaze locked onto the boys' hands. Both of them were carrying enormous green ice cream cones!

Jamal licked his, a blissful expression on his face. "This is the best ice cream cone I've ever tasted," he said with a sigh. "The flavors sound really weird, but they taste amazing!"

Rachel and Kirsty exchanged a glance.

"Did you buy them from Charlie?" Kirsty asked, pointing at the truck behind them.

"No," Liam replied, "they're from that truck over there — the bright green one.

All of their ice cream is green, too!" Hidden in Rachel's pocket, Esme gave a squeak of excitement. Both girls knew why. The green ice cream truck must be connected with the goblins!

"Thanks," said Kirsty. "Come on,

Rachel. Let's go there right now!"

With a wave to the boys, the girls raced off. If they could find the goblins, maybe they could find Esme's magic charm, too!

A Cool Pool?

There was a long line stretching back from the green ice cream truck, and the girls joined the end. Everyone walking away with their bright green ice cream cones was exclaiming how delicious they were.

"Look—we were right," whispered

Rachel. "There are goblins in the truck!"

Kirsty and Esme looked over. The three ice cream sellers in the truck were dressed in uniforms like Charlie's, except they were bright green. They wore hats over their eyes. But even the hats couldn't disguise what long noses they all had . . . and how green their skin was!

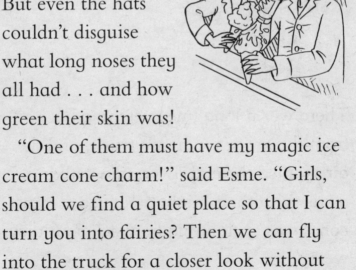

"One of them must have my magic ice cream cone charm!" said Esme. "Girls, should we find a quiet place so that I can turn you into fairies? Then we can fly into the truck for a closer look without anyone seeing us."

"Yes, please," Kirsty said at once.
Being a fairy was always so much fun!

Rachel and Kirsty left the line and hid behind a truck selling cups of tea and coffee. There, Esme waved her wand and murmured some magic words. A swirl of bright stars and sparkles flooded from her wand and whirled around the girls. They immediately shrank smaller and smaller until they were the same size as Esme! Then they fluttered off the ground with their very own shimmering, gauzy wings.

"Thank you!" Rachel cried, twirling in midair.

"Let's investigate," Kirsty said, zooming high. "Come on!"

The three fairies flew above the crowd as they headed for the green ice cream truck. The back door was open, so they zipped inside and hid on a shelf behind a huge tub of green ice cream. Peeking out, they could see the three goblins working at the counter.

"There you go," said the first goblin to a customer, handing over two cones of green ice cream decorated with green fudge sauce. "Who's next?"

"This is the best job ever," the second

30

goblin said. He was making an ice
cream sundae, decorated with green
whipped cream. He paused to squirt
whipped cream into his mouth. "Yum!"
he said happily.

"We shouldn't use all the ice cream,
remember," the third goblin said bossily.
"We have to keep enough for Jack Frost's
Candy Castle."

"That's right—he's going to fill his swimming pool with ice cream!" the first goblin said, adding green sprinkles to another cone. "How cool is that?" He chuckled suddenly. "Cool—ice cream. Get it?"

The fairies exchanged glances as the goblins laughed.

"I wouldn't want to swim in ice cream," Rachel whispered, shivering. "Think how cold it would be."

"And sticky," Kirsty said, wrinkling her nose.

Esme looked upset. "Ice cream isn't meant for *swimming* in,"

32

she said. "It's for cones and sundaes and milkshakes. What is Jack Frost thinking?"

"It's such a waste, too," Rachel agreed. "Especially when the fairies need ice cream for Treat Day. We need to find your magic charm fast, and stop all this craziness!"

Turning Green

While the girls were talking, the goblins
had started bickering. "The ice cream
pool should be Spinach Swirl flavor," the
first goblin said.

"No way—Broccoli Chunk is the
best," the second goblin argued, squirting
more whipped cream into his mouth.

"You two don't know what you're
talking about," the third added.

"Cabbage Surprise
is the tastiest.
Imagine
jumping off
the diving board
and landing
headfirst
in *that*!"

"Diving board?
There isn't going to be
a diving board," scoffed the first goblin.
"I heard Jack Frost was putting one of
those superfast water slides in the pool.
It's going to be awesome!"

While the goblins squabbled, Kirsty,
Rachel, and Esme began quietly
searching through the truck. It was
stocked with lots of different flavors of

ice cream (all green) plus green sprinkles, green sauces, green cones, green cherries, and green chocolate flakes. Searching through everything was nerve-racking —especially since the goblins were so close and kept turning around to use different toppings and sauces! Both Kirsty and Rachel had to move very quickly more than once so that they wouldn't be spotted.

Unfortunately, after searching high and low, there was no sign of

Esme's magic ice cream cone charm anywhere.

"I don't understand," Esme sighed as they fluttered back to the shelf. "We've looked everywhere! Where could it be?"

"Maybe one of the goblins is wearing it on a chain around his neck," Kirsty suggested. Each fairy flew to a different goblin, perched lightly on his shoulder, and peered carefully down his collar. They didn't see any chains, though.

"Do they have pockets on their

uniforms?" Esme wondered. "Maybe one goblin has the charm hidden in a pocket."

It took only a moment for them to realize that the goblins didn't have any pockets on their jackets, so the magic charm couldn't be there, either.

Just as they were starting to feel stumped, Rachel's eye was caught by the goblins' paper hats. She remembered how Esme had been hiding in one earlier. "Maybe the charm is underneath one of their hats," she whispered. "But which one?"

Kirsty thought for a moment. "I have an idea," she said with a smile. "Follow me."

Kirsty flitted out of the back door with Esme and Rachel close behind, and explained her plan.

"The goblins are arguing so much already, I bet we can persuade them to have a food fight with the ice cream.

And then their hats are sure to be
knocked off!" she said.

"I love it," Esme said.
"But how can
we encourage
them to have a
food fight?"
Rachel
grinned. "By
starting one ourselves,"
she suggested. "Could
you use your magic to disguise us as
goblin ice cream sellers, Esme? We could
set a very bad example for them. . . ."

Esme's eyes twinkled. "Perfect," she
said. "I'll just get rid of this crowd of
people first. I would hate for any of them
to get splattered!"

Esme tapped herself lightly on the head

with her wand
and murmured
a magic spell.
Then she began
to speak, but
her words came
out much louder
than usual. In fact,
she sounded exactly
like a loudspeaker
announcement!

"Ladies and gentlemen," she boomed.
"I regret to inform you that the Bright
Green Ice Cream Machine has now run
out of ice cream, and we are no longer
able to serve you. We apologize for any
inconvenience."

A sigh of dismay went up from the

crowd that had gathered around the
truck. The goblins were still arguing,
and didn't even notice their line
wandering away!

Esme tapped her head again, breaking
the spell on her voice. "There—now for
part two of the plan," she said with a
mischievous smile. "Two new ice cream
sellers!"

She waved her
wand, and a
flurry of magic
sparkles flew
around Kirsty
and Rachel.
The girls
grew bigger
and greener,

43

with pointy noses and big ears.

Rachel giggled at the sight of her and Kirsty. They looked just like the goblins, and had trays of ice cream hanging around their necks. "We definitely look nicer as fairies than goblins!" she said.

"I don't feel very dainty anymore, with these enormous feet," Kirsty agreed with a grin. She adjusted her tray of ice cream. "But never mind. We have a plan to try out. Let's hope it works!"

splat!

Rachel took a deep breath as she and Kirsty walked out around the front of the truck. She knew that Esme's magic wouldn't last long. They only had a few minutes before their goblin disguises wore off. They had to get this right!

Kirsty gave Rachel a wink, then launched right into their plan. "You did

it again, didn't you?" she said in a loud, angry voice. "I TOLD you not to keep eating the ice cream. We're supposed to be taking it back to Jack Frost, remember?"

"I know that!" Rachel snapped. "And it's not ME who's been eating the ice cream, anyway. It must be you!" With that, she grabbed a scoop of ice cream from a tub left on the counter by a lazy goblin.

The ice cream flew through the air, knocking Kirsty's hat off.

"How dare you?" Kirsty cried, pretending to be outraged. "Take THAT!" She grabbed a nearby stack of cones and threw them back at Rachel.

As she bent to pick up her hat, Kirsty saw the goblins' faces light up with glee. Goblins could never resist a fight! Within moments, they had all joined the food fight—hurling ice cream, sprinkles,

and cherries at one another. One goblin
even used the can of whipped cream like
a water pistol, squirting the other goblins
in the face.

Rachel and Kirsty grinned. Their plan
was working! They each grabbed more
ice cream and began hurling lumps of it
into the truck.

Splat! One lump knocked off the first goblin's paper hat . . . but nothing was hidden underneath.

Splat! Kirsty had to aim high since the next goblin was tall, but the gooey scoop she threw sent his hat flying, too. She held her breath as it fell . . . but his head was bare beneath it.

Now there was only one goblin left wearing a hat. Kirsty and Rachel both took careful aim. *Splat! Splat!* Kirsty's

scoop of ice cream just missed, hitting him on the ear and sliding down his neck. Rachel's scoop, however, was a direct hit, and sent his paper hat flying! Underneath was a small pink and gold ice cream cone charm, sparkling as it lay on the goblin's head!

"Quick, Esme!" whispered Rachel in delight.

Hiding in Rachel's pocket, Esme had seen everything. She darted out like a bright ember of light, flying straight for the magic charm.

Just as Esme was about to reach out and grab it, one of the other goblins

noticed her. "Hey, watch out! There's a sneaky fairy in here!" he cried, swatting at Esme with his ice cream scoop.

"She's after the magic cone!" the tall goblin realized. He snatched the charm off the third goblin's head and dashed out of the truck as fast as he could.

53

Rachel opened her mouth to shout "After him!" but remembered at the last second that she was still disguised as a goblin. Instead, she cried, "Don't worry, I'll catch that fairy!" and ran behind Esme, who was already flying after the tall goblin.

Kirsty joined her. "Come back here!" she yelled. Really, both girls hoped Esme would catch up with the tall goblin. Unfortunately, he was a fast runner and showed no sign of slowing down.

"He's getting away," Rachel realized with a groan as they raced along behind the goblin and Esme.

"And our plan had been working so well!" Kirsty sighed. "Now what are we going to do?"

Trapped!

"The goblin's too fast! I don't think Esme can catch him," Rachel said. "Unless he ends up in a dead end somewhere. . . ."

Kirsty grinned. "Wouldn't it be awful if his goblin friends sent him the wrong way?" she said with a wink. "There's an alley just off the main road that's a dead end. Let's try to send him down there."

"Genius!" Rachel smiled, then called ahead to the goblin. "There's a shortcut on your left!" she yelled. "You can get away from the fairy if you go that way."

He glanced back, saw Rachel—still disguised as a goblin—and gave her a thumbs-up. Then he ducked down the alley, with Esme, Kirsty, and Rachel all following him.

Of course, the alley wasn't a shortcut at all— it ended in a high brick wall. There was no escape! The goblin spun around. "This isn't a shortcut!" he yelled. His

eyes widened at the sight of Esme darting toward him. "Now what?"

"Throw the charm to me, I'll keep it safe!" Rachel called.

Thinking she was a goblin, the tall goblin did just that. Rachel deftly caught the charm and held it out on her palm for Esme.

The goblin's jaw dropped as Esme flew down to take it. In the next second, the girls' goblin disguises wore off.

"You tricked me!" the goblin wailed, stamping his foot. "No fair!" The other two goblins had caught up now, panting and clutching their sides. They groaned when they realized what had happened. "And we used up almost all the ice cream in our food fight," one of them complained nervously. "Jack Frost is going to be so angry!"

The goblins looked so worried, the girls felt a little sorry for them. "It's not your fault that Jack Frost is so greedy," Kirsty said.

"Nobody needs an ice cream swimming pool," Rachel added.

Esme smiled. "Do you think an ice cream *bath* would be OK, instead?" she asked, twirling her wand. Suddenly, a large white bathtub on wheels appeared . . . filled with glittering green ice cream!

The goblins looked much more cheerful. "Thank you," they said, and

wheeled the bathtub away down the
alley.

Esme fastened her magic charm
bracelet around her wrist. A sudden
bright flash of light sparked in the air.
"There," she said happily. "Now ice
cream everywhere should be super-tasty
again."

Rachel grinned. "Well, there's only one
way to find out," she said. "Come on,
let's pay another visit to Charlie."

The three friends went back down the alley. To their delight, they saw that Charlie had opened his ice cream truck again and had a long line of customers waiting eagerly.

"Hooray!" Esme cheered at the sight. "Thank you both so much. I'd better go back to Fairyland now to work on my new flavors for Treat Day. Enjoy your ice cream!"

"I'm sure we will," Kirsty said. She and Rachel watched Esme fly away until she was just a tiny dot in the sky. Then she vanished! The girls joined Charlie's line.

After all that running, they felt awfully hungry!

It took a while for Rachel and Kirsty to reach the front of the line, but when it was finally their turn, they noticed two new flavors on the display board. "Ooh, Strawberry Sparkle sounds good," Kirsty said, opening her purse.

"And I'd like the Marshmallow Magic flavor, please," Rachel said.

Charlie smiled and handed over their ice cream cones. Just as he went to serve the next customer, a pinch of glittery sprinkles appeared on their ice cream, and the girls beamed. They knew the sprinkles were a gift from Esme. Fairy magic was so wonderful!

Rachel and Kirsty walked away, licking their ice cream. "*Mmm*," Rachel said. "Marshmallow Magic is absolutely delicious."

"So is Strawberry Sparkle," Kirsty said happily. Then she remembered something. "Oh — and we still have Aunt Helen's surprise for us back at home! I wonder what it is."

"One thing's for sure," Rachel said as they walked along. "With all of these Sugar and Spice Fairy adventures, we're in for a tasty time!"

THE SUGAR AND SPICE FAIRIES

Rachel and Kirsty found Lisa and Esme's missing
magic charms. Now it's time for them to help

Coco

the Cupcake Fairy!

Join their next adventure in this
special sneak peek. . . .

A Sweet
Surprise

"This has been such an exciting day,"
said Rachel Walker, licking her
Marshmallow Magic ice cream. "We've
already been to Fairyland *and* helped
two fairies get their magic charms back
from Jack Frost."

Rachel and her best friend, Kirsty
Tate, were walking home from the
Wetherbury village square, where they

had been looking around the market. Rachel was visiting Kirsty for spring break, and it looked like they were going to have an exciting week.

"The day's not over yet," added Kirsty, smiling. She paused to lick her Strawberry Sparkle ice cream, which was melting in the hazy afternoon sun and running over her fingers. "I have a feeling that now that magical things have *started* happening, they're going to *keep* happening!" she went on, licking her fingers one by one.

No one in the human world knew that the girls had been on many adventures in Fairyland. They were always excited to make new fairy friends and help outwit Jack Frost and his naughty goblins. That morning, Honey the Candy Fairy had

visited them to ask for help again. This
time, Jack Frost and his goblins had
stolen the seven magic charms belonging
to the Sugar and Spice Fairies. Without
them, all of the candy and treats in both
the human world and Fairyland were
ruined!

"We've already rescued Lisa the
Lollipop Fairy's magic lollipop charm
and Esme the Ice Cream Fairy's magic
ice cream cone charm," Rachel said,
chewing on a deliciously sticky
marshmallow. "But there are still five
more charms to find."

"And if we don't find them fast,
Fairyland's Treat Day will be ruined!"
said Kirsty, biting her lip.

The day after tomorrow was Treat
Day in Fairyland. King Oberon and

Queen Titania always gave a basket of special treats to each fairy to thank them for their hard work all year. But Jack Frost was using the Sugar and Spice Fairies' magic charms to get all the treats for himself. There weren't any left for the fairies! He was planning to build a giant Candy Castle, and he had given the magic charms to his goblins for safekeeping.

The goblins had come to the human world to find even *more* treats to steal for the Candy Castle. Rachel and Kirsty kept a careful lookout for the little green troublemakers as they walked past the village hall. They knew that goblins could pop up anywhere!